PRESCOTT PUBLIC LIBRARY
3 1449 00157 0151

D0570055

THE TETON SIOUX INDIANS

THE JUNIOR LIBRARY OF
AMERICAN INDIANS

THE TETON SIOUX INDIANS

Terrance Dolan

CHELSEA JUNIORS

a division of CHELSEA HOUSE PUBLISHERS

FRONTISPIECE: Teton Sioux chief Sitting Bull.

CHAPTER TITLE ORNAMENT: An elk similar to one drawn on a shield that probably belonged to a member of the Elk Dreamer society.

English-language words that are italicized in the text can be found in the glossary at the back of the book.

Chelsea House Publishers
EDITORIAL DIRECTOR Richard Rennert
EXECUTIVE MANAGING EDITOR Karyn Gullen Browne
COPY CHIEF Robin James
PICTURE EDITOR Adrian G. Allen
ART DIRECTOR Robert Mitchell
MANUFACTURING DIRECTOR Gerald Levine

The Junior Library of American Indians
SENIOR EDITOR Martin Schwabacher

Staff for THE TETON SIOUX INDIANS
ASSOCIATE EDITOR David Shirley
COPY EDITOR Catherine Iannone
EDITORIAL ASSISTANT Annie McDonnell
ASSISTANT DESIGNER John Infantino
PICTURE RESEARCHER Sandy Jones
COVER ILLUSTRATOR Shelley Pritchett

First Printing

1 3 5 7 9 8 6 4 2

Library of Congress Cataloging-in-Publication Data

Dolan, Terrance.
The Teton Sioux Indians/Terrance Dolan.
p. cm.—(The Junior library of American Indians)
Includes index.
ISBN 0-7910-1680-3
ISBN 0-7910-2032-0 (pbk.)
1. Teton Indians—History—Juvenile literature. 2. Teton Indians—Social life and customs—Juvenile literature. [1. Teton Indians. 2. Indians of North America.] I. Title. II. Series.
E99.T34D65 1994 94-7167
973'.04975—dc20 CIP
AC

CONTENTS

CHAPTER 1
Strong Medicine 7

CHAPTER 2
Preparing for War 17

CHAPTER 3
Thunder Moon 27

CHAPTER 4
Wakan Tanka 39

PICTURE ESSAY
The Sacred and the Mundane 41

CHAPTER 5
"You Will Have To Fight the Sioux Warriors" 55

CHAPTER 6
The Heart of Crazy Horse 67

Glossary 76

Chronology 77

Index 78

Chief Black Rock was a proud leader of the Teton Sioux, one of the most powerful and respected tribes of the Great Plains.

CHAPTER 1

Strong Medicine

When white Americans and the Teton Sioux first interacted with one another, the word *medicine* was often used. Communication between whites and Indians was difficult. They spoke vastly different languages. A simple word such as *medicine* might be adopted by both peoples to represent a certain idea. When white Americans and Indians were communicating, and they spoke of medicine, they were talking about something that was much different from what we mean today when we use the same word.

When used by Indians, *medicine* meant a kind of spiritual presence and power. The Teton Sioux—along with all the other original

American tribes and nations—were spiritual people. Medicine was an essential part of their life and the way they saw things. Many white Americans believed that *medicine* simply meant "Indian magic." But for native Americans, *medicine* was a far richer and more meaningful concept. When the Teton Sioux used this term, it represented the spiritual life-force that inhabited all things. Medicine was the presence of *Wakan Tanka*—the Creator and Great Spirit.

Medicine *is the Sioux word for the magical power hidden in ordinary people, places, and things. Medicine men, such as Blue Medicine (pictured here), played an important role in the day-to-day life of the Teton Sioux.*

According to the Teton Sioux, everything in the world had medicine—people, creatures, objects, actions, even words and ideas. Some things had more powerful medicine than others. The spark of Wakan Tanka glowed brightly within them. These things were said to be strong medicine. For example, the buffalo, wolf, and grizzly bear were strong medicine. A brave warrior or gifted healer was strong medicine. A specific place might be strong medicine. Certain *rituals* were strong medicine. Objects, especially those used in spiritual rituals and ceremonies, might be strong medicine. And as both white people and Indians agreed—the Teton Sioux were strong medicine.

Originally, the Sioux (pronounced like the name Sue) lived in the forests of Minnesota and Wisconsin. In their early days, they were not the powerful nation they became on the northern Great Plains. In Minnesota and Wisconsin, they were continually *harassed* by such eastern tribes as the Chippewas and the huge, warlike Iroquois Confederacy. These people, especially the Iroquois, had many guns, which they had obtained from French and English hunters and fur traders who had come to North America from Europe. The Sioux had very little contact with white people at this point. Without the guns that the white settlers provided, the Sioux were unable to compete with their enemies in battle. So they moved away from them, toward the west.

As they migrated westward, the main body of Sioux split up. The Santee Sioux, also known as the Dakota Sioux, settled in the woodlands on the western edge of Minnesota. The Yankton Sioux, also known as the Nakota Sioux, remained east of the Missouri River in South Dakota. The Teton Sioux, who called themselves the *Lakotas,* continued westward. They crossed the Missouri River in South Dakota around 1735.

The northern Great Plains of South and North Dakota, northern Nebraska, Montana, and Wyoming were a different world from the Minnesota and Wisconsin woodlands. The Teton Sioux believed that their people first appeared on earth when they were led from a deep cave by a wolf. Emerging from the dense, shadowy forests of Minnesota and Wisconsin onto the Great Plains must have seemed like emerging from a cave onto the surface of the earth. Instead of forest, the Sioux now found themselves trekking across a vast, awe-inspiring ocean of rolling prairie. Directly eastward, the plains ended where they met the sky at the horizon, so far in the distance that it looked like the edge of the world.

To the west, the northern Great Plains were broken only by a dark mountain range. These hills were blanketed with heavy forest. In contrast to the pale green and brown of the prairie, the hills appeared to be black. They were known as *Paha-Sapa*—the Black Hills. The Teton Sioux headed in the direction of the Black Hills.

The immensity of the Great Plains is overwhelming. The first Europeans to venture onto the Great Plains were Spanish conquistadores in the 16th century. The conquistadores were the most fearless group of adventurers to reach the shores of the New World, but on the plains the Spanish settlers felt tiny and insignificant. The bold conquistadores were not accustomed to feeling tiny and insignificant. This made them nervous.

They were more than happy to leave the Great Plains behind.

Like other Europeans, the conquistadores did not view the natural world in the same manner as the Teton Sioux. White settlers attempted to *impose* themselves on the natural environment. They tried to make it as *un*natural as possible. They considered themselves to be above nature. They felt that the natural world was something to be mastered.

Original Americans such as the Teton Sioux had an entirely different point of view. Instead of attempting to force the natural environment to adapt to them, they adapted to the natural environment. They became part of it. They joined the cycles and rhythms of nature, the four seasons and four winds, the rolling hills and grasslands—the earth. To attempt to master the natural environment would be the same as attempting to master Wakan Tanka. This was unthinkable. Through rituals and sacrifices, the Sioux could appeal to Wakan Tanka for power or guidance. But no human could master Wakan Tanka.

The Teton Sioux adapted to the plains. Eventually they considered themselves a part of the plains—along with the buffalo, the wolf, the coyote, the bear, and the elk. But

the Teton Sioux felt that these creatures were superior to humans. The presence of these animals allowed the Teton Sioux to survive. Nothing that a human could do, on the other hand, made existence easier for these creatures.

Observing the ways of the wolf, the Teton Sioux knew that this creature was greater

Before the arrival of white settlers, great hordes of buffalo roamed the plains of the American heartland. The meat and hides of the massive beasts were crucial to the welfare of the Teton Sioux.

medicine than any human. The wolf was closer to nature. Therefore, the wolf contained a brighter spark of the spirit of Wakan Tanka. The natural world was filled with the presence and power of Wakan Tanka. And yet a wolf might be killed by a Sioux arrow. If this happened, the Teton Sioux understood that the wolf had sacrificed itself for their well-being.

The Teton Sioux were a deeply spiritual people. Their spirituality was not something that was practiced on a certain day for a period of time and then put aside. Some important Teton Sioux spiritual ceremonies and rituals took place at specific times and places. But the Teton Sioux did not separate their spirituality from day-to-day life on the plains. The various activities and events of everyday life held spiritual significance.

Unlike many religions, Teton Sioux spirituality was not a way of explaining the universe. The Sioux often spoke of the universe and Wakan Tanka as the Great Mysterious. For the Teton Sioux, spirituality was an awareness of the sacred nature of all things. It was also a way of interacting with the universe. The Teton Sioux did not feel that they had a particularly special place in the Great Mysterious. In fact, they considered themselves to be a very small and insignificant part of the universe. They simply were grateful that Wakan Tanka provided the things on which the Teton Sioux depended for survival. And they depended on nothing so much as *Tatanka*—the buffalo.

The buffalo was truly a blessing to the Teton Sioux and the other tribes of the Great Plains. Here, in this harsh and often unforgiving land, roamed countless numbers of these big, shaggy creatures. They thundered across the grasslands in herds of unimaginable size. The buffalo provided the Teton Sioux with virtually everything they needed.

The buffalo gave the Teton Sioux fresh meat, and enough extra meat to be preserved and eaten throughout the winter. The tongue and bone marrow were delicious delicacies. Blood was used to make a thick soup. The heavily furred hide of the front portion of the buffalo was made into buffalo robes. *Tipis* and lodges were also made from the hides, as were war shields. Bones were fashioned into tools, hooks, needles, cooking utensils, and weapons. Horns were made into spoons and drinking cups. The top of the skull was a fine bowl. The bladder was used as a water pouch. Hooves were crushed into powders to be used in medicines. Sinew, tendons, and muscle served as rope and thread. Brains, liver, and fat were used to treat and soften the hides during the making of robes and tipis. (Boiled buffalo brains were quite tasty as well.) The tail was an excellent fly swatter. These were just some of the uses the Teton Sioux found for the buffalo.

Because the buffalo provided so much of itself for the well-being of the Teton Sioux, it was the most honored and respected of all the creatures of the plains. White men viewed the buffalo as a dumb, slow, clumsy beast that hardly knew enough to run away when a rifle was pointed at its head. For the Teton Sioux, Father Buffalo was powerful medicine. Tatanka was the most ancient, wise, and generous inhabitant of the plains. The image or symbol of Tatanka dominated most Teton Sioux spiritual rituals, dances, songs, and ceremonies.

A child who was spoken to by Tatanka in a dream was a Buffalo Dreamer. This child was destined to become a *shaman*, or medicine man. Shamans developed spiritual wisdom. They possessed powers, such as the ability to heal the sick and wounded or to see future events. The Teton Sioux hunted and killed the buffalo, but they understood that in truth they were the guests of the buffalo. Without the generosity of Tatanka, the Teton Sioux could not survive on the Great Plains.

The Teton Sioux obtained their horses by capturing them from wild herds and by raiding the stock of other tribes. The speedy animals allowed Sioux hunters and warriors to travel great distances in a short period of time.

CHAPTER 2

Preparing for War

The Sioux were newcomers to the northern Great Plains. Other tribes were already well established in this region. Many of them—such as the Crows, Arikaras, Pawnees, Shoshones, and Kiowas—were warlike and fierce. Wars, battles, and sudden raids were a way of life among the tribes of the plains. The established tribes did little to welcome the new arrivals, and the Teton Sioux lived in constant fear of attack. As they migrated westward across the plains, however, the Teton Sioux acquired two things that put them on equal footing with these hostile peoples—the horse and the gun.

The Teton Sioux obtained horses by capturing them from wild herds and by raiding other tribes. The Sioux prized pintos above all other horses. Pintos were small, swift, durable, and nimble. They could go at a full gallop for miles without tiring. Once a wild pinto was tamed, it became highly responsive to a skilled rider. A pinto could be brought to a full halt and spurred back to a full gallop within a moment. They turned quickly and sharply. The Teton Sioux loved their beautiful coloring. A pinto with especially eye-catching splotches of color was prized. The pintos were ideal for the two primary activities of the Plains peoples—buffalo hunting and warfare.

The Sioux had a large arsenal of traditional weapons of war. Among these were bows and arrows, hatchets, whips, knives, lances, and spiked clubs. To these, the Sioux soon added guns. They began acquiring these from other tribes and from traders who were making their way onto the northern plains in the mid-1700s. Having been pushed from their original lands, the Teton Sioux did not intend to be pushed again. Now they would do the pushing.

The Teton Sioux were physically large and strong compared to many other Plains peoples. They were expert in the use of the bow and arrow. They soon became masterful horsemen and skilled marksmen with firearms. But as the Teton Sioux battled the other tribes of the high plains, it was their sheer courage and ferocity as much as anything else that enabled them to defeat these tribes and to drive them away.

On the night before a battle, Teton Sioux warriors held war dances until dawn. They then dressed in their finest battle attire—buffalo-bone breastplates, colorful feather headdresses, special shirts and leggings—all strikingly painted and adorned. Many of their deerskin and elk-skin shirts had the scalps of slain enemy warriors sewn into them. Leggings or shirts might have a fringe of human hair.

Teton Sioux warriors painted their faces and their horses with bold, frightening symbols, streaks, and patterns. Many warriors rode into battle virtually naked but with their entire body painted in streaks of red, yellow, or blue. Their shields and weapons were colorfully painted and decorated with feathers. The Teton Sioux warriors twisted their long black hair into braids and secured the braids with otter-skin ties. "Today is a good day to die," some would sing as they rode into battle.

The Teton Sioux were utterly fearless, and they inspired great fear in their enemies.

Teton Sioux warriors were utterly fearless in battle, and their courage and daring were highly respected by other tribes. Here, a band of Sioux warriors prepares for a surprise attack on a Crow village.

They learned to imitate the roar of an enraged grizzly bear, the most fearsome creature on the continent. Growling like a horde of grizzlies, they met their foes. Despite their guns and bows and arrows, Teton Sioux warriors always attempted to make physical contact with their enemies, even if they had to ride or run directly into their midst. To make physical contact with an enemy warrior represented the utmost in courage for the Teton Sioux. This was known as *counting coup.* It did not matter if the enemy was killed or injured. Simply riding or charging through a rain of arrows and bullets and giving an enemy warrior a whack with a coup stick was good enough. It was the act of boldness and courage, rather than the act of injuring or killing, that mattered. On the other hand, the Teton Sioux killed plenty of enemy fighters as well. The mighty Teton Sioux warrior Gall, for example, was known for counting coup on the heads of his enemies with an extremely large hatchet.

Many Sioux men belonged to *Akicita* societies such as the Kit Foxes, the Badgers, the Strong Hearts, or the Crow Owners.

The Akicitas were warrior societies. Akicita officers often dismounted in the heat of battle. These warriors wore an honorary sash tied around their waist. Taking off the sash, they tied one end to a lance and the other around their ankle. They then drove the lance deep into the ground. There, unable to move beyond the length of the sash, they stood and fought. They could not, and did not, release themselves until the battle was over, even if their war party was in retreat. They could only be released by a fellow member of their Akicita society. When this did happen, it was quite disappointing to the warrior who had staked himself to the ground.

The Teton Sioux became renowned for their *stoicism* when experiencing great pain. White men who battled the Teton Sioux were

Teton Sioux braves took part in ceremonial initiation rites to prove their bravery. Often, this meant enduring great pain for long periods of time.

particularly amazed by this quality. Pierced by an arrow, a Teton Sioux warrior might simply pull it out and continue fighting. (He might not even bother to pull it out.) A Sioux with a terrible wound could often be seen calmly leading his pony from the battleground. The warrior's face displayed no pain or emotion. He did not cry out or utter a sound. He walked for a while, sat down, sang his death song, and died. Others might return to camp. There, they were treated by the women and healers. Teton Sioux warriors often recovered from wounds that seemed fatal.

Some Teton Sioux had a different sort of medicine. For years, the legendary warrior Crazy Horse fought in many of the bloodiest battles to be waged on the Great Plains. Yet he was never touched by a bullet or an arrow. Crazy Horse enjoyed acting as a decoy. In order to lure an enemy force into an ambush, he rode into plain sight, well within the range of the enemy's rifles or bows. While the enemy blazed away at him, Crazy Horse calmly dismounted and pretended to examine his pinto's hooves, or to adjust his moccasins. Bullets and arrows flew about him but Crazy Horse remained untouched. He would then climb back on his pinto and ride away. His frustrated enemies would follow—usually into an ambush. Crazy Horse was strong medicine.

One by one, the Teton Sioux fought the tribes of the northern plains—the Pawnees, the Arikaras, the Shoshones, the Crees, the Ojibwas, the Poncas, and the Omahas. Steadily, the Sioux pushed these tribes away to the north, south, east, and west. At the same time, the Sioux became allies with the Cheyennes and the Arapahos, two fierce tribes of the northern plains. In 1795, after 10 years of fighting, the Teton Sioux and their allies finally dislodged the stubborn Kiowas from the Black Hills. The Teton Sioux then continued their expansion westward into Montana and Wyoming. Early in the 1800s, they took control of the Bighorn Mountains of Montana and Wyoming from the numerous and powerful Crows.

As they acquired more and more territory on the northern plains, the Teton Sioux divided into seven tribes—known as the *Seven Council Fires.* Each division became known by a certain name and patrolled a specific territory. Brulé Sioux territory included northern Nebraska and southern South Dakota. The Two Kettles' division was located just west of the Missouri River in South Dakota. Miniconjou Sioux territory encompassed central and northern South Dakota. Farther north were the Hunkpapa, Sans Arc, and Blackfeet Sioux. Oglala Sioux territory included a vast area of western South Dakota, southeastern Montana, and northeastern Wyoming. At the heart of the territory of the Seven Council Fires were the Black Hills.

By the mid-1800s, the tribe that had been pushed by enemies onto the northern plains had become the Teton Sioux Nation. They controlled a large portion of the northern region of the American West. This vast area offered the best hunting grounds of the entire Great Plains. With the decline of the Iroquois Confederacy of the Northeast, the Teton Sioux were now the most powerful Indian nation in North America. ▲

During the hunting season, the Teton Sioux followed the great herds of buffalo around the plains. Entire villages might be moved several times during a single season.

CHAPTER 3

Thunder Moon

During the summer months, the Teton Sioux lived a *nomadic* existence, as bands of *tiyospes* followed the buffalo herds across the plains. Tiyospes were the family groups of Teton Sioux society. A tiyospe was led by a headman—a strong, wise hunter and warrior. The tiyospe usually included the headman's wife or wives, their children, and the headman's parents and grandparents. The headman's in-laws and their parents, along with the headman's brothers and sisters, were often part of his tiyospe. If brothers or sisters were married, their husbands, wives, and children might join the headman's tiyospe as well. Cousins, close friends of the headman, and adopted children might also belong to a headman's tiyospe.

A tiyospe traveled together, hunted together, ate together, and camped together in clusters of lodges and tipis among a larger band of their people. It was good to have a large tiyospe. This provided more males to kill buffalo for food, to raid the Crow, Pawnee, or Shoshone tribes for horses, and to defend the camp against raids.

A large tiyospe also had more females to accomplish many essential and difficult tasks. These tasks included the making of buffalo robes, elk-skin or deerskin leggings and shirts, and tipis. Women decorated clothing by quilling and painting. (Quilling was a delicate art form in which women used thread made from buffalo sinew to sew designs of colorfully painted porcupine quills into clothing.) Women crafted bead and bear-claw necklaces and chokers, quilled armlets, and made other fashionable items such as coin earrings. In addition to all this, Sioux women were expected to gather berries and herbs, to cook, and to perform many other duties.

Everyone in a tiyospe took part in raising the children. Children were treasured by the Teton Sioux. They were never hit or spanked, and adults never yelled at them. A child in a large tiyospe had many "mothers" and "fathers." Grandparents formed special bonds with young children. The elderly Sioux helped to take care of the children and to teach them, using the knowledge they had acquired during their long lives.

The rise to power of the Teton Sioux was not simply a result of their success as hunters and warriors. Teton Sioux society was communal. The community, rather than the individual, was all-important. This gave the Teton Sioux society inner strength. A Teton Sioux warrior who captured 10 horses from the Crows, for example, won praise for his exploit. But even greater respect was reserved for the brave warrior who then gave some of his horses to others who did not have as many, or to those who had none at all. This warrior had strengthened the well-being of the entire community.

Among the Teton Sioux, generosity was as highly respected as bravery. A Teton Sioux warrior who had performed heroically in battle celebrated by giving gifts to members of the community. Newlyweds celebrated their marriage by giving gifts, instead of receiving them. A young man celebrated his acceptance into an Akicita society by giving away horses. It was the responsibility of the individual to share his or her good fortune, happiness, and wealth with the community through acts of generosity. In this manner, Teton Sioux society formed a spirit of unity. The importance of the overall well-being of the community was constantly reinforced. And this, in turn, made the community strong and healthy.

The biggest event of the summer was the Sun Dance. The Sun Dance was the most important of all Teton Sioux spiritual ceremonies. It was held during July, the month known as Moon of the Ripening Chokeberries. The Seven Council Fires gathered for this ceremony. The Sun Dance was a 12-day celebration of the entire Teton Sioux Nation.

During the Sun Dance ritual itself, participants attached themselves to a tall cottonwood Sun Dance pole by using rawhide ropes with sharpened sticks at the end of each rope. Sun Dancers inserted the sticks through a thin opening that was cut into the skin of their upper chest or back. A Sun Dancer's friend or a respected shaman or warrior would often do this for him. A dancer's sister or sisters, or a wife or future wife, wiped away the blood and soothed the wound with fresh grass. The other end of the rope was fastened to the top of the pole. The length of the rope forced the dancer to

The Teton Sioux developed a complex and efficient form of village life that enhanced the welfare of all of the members of the tribe.

stand. Even then, the rope was stretched tight, pulling the dancer upward. A buffalo skull was placed within the ring of dancers, facing the pole. The Sun Dancers then danced and prayed to *Wi*, the sun god. A Sun Dancer might dance for an entire day, staring directly into the sun.

The ritual was grueling and painful, and only the most dedicated men endured it. Despite the pain, Sun Dancers did not cry out or utter any sound of discomfort. Through their sacrifice to Wi, the Sun Dancers brought the blessing of Wakan Tanka onto the entire Teton Sioux Nation. A man who participated in the Sun Dance won much respect from all the Teton Sioux. Sun Dance scars allowed a Sioux to carry himself with great pride.

The Sun Dance ritual was preceded and followed by many feasts, ceremonies, and general socializing. Many gifts were given. Young men and women from the seven tribes met and fell in love. Marriages were arranged. Friends and relatives who had not seen one another for a long time were joyfully reunited. After 12 days, the seven tribes departed. All the members of the Teton Sioux Nation felt the strong medicine of the Sun Dance. And the Seven Council Fires were strengthened as a nation and as a single community.

In the autumn, all the tiyospes of a tribe joined together for the *wani-sapa*—the big hunt. Having killed enough buffalo and other animals during the big hunt to last the winter, many bands of Teton Sioux tiyospes journeyed to the Black Hills to make winter camp.

Once a band of tiyospes arrived in the Black Hills, a village of lodges and tipis would spring up. Usually, a winter camp was situated in a deep valley by a stream. There, the camp was sheltered from the sweeping, icy blasts of wind that roared across the Great Plains in the winter and the blizzards that turned the entire world into a swirling whiteness. The Black Hills divided the winds that howled around and over them. The winds were weakened by the many trees that covered the hills. The trees also captured the heavy snows. And the trees provided plenty of firewood for the long winter.

But even the Black Hills did not guarantee a safe winter. Food might run short if the fall hunt had been poor. Or *Gnaske*, the Crazy Buffalo, might thump through the camp one night. This could cause insanity to take hold of a member of the tiyospe. Or a Sioux who ventured out into the snows at night to gather fresh firewood might encounter the monstrous *Unktehi*, who would transform him into a rabbit or a dog. A Sioux woman whose husband went out into the forest and did not return for a long time had good reason to worry. Late that night, or at dawn, if a strange dog came scratching at the tipi flaps, or a rabbit hopped in, the wife began to

mourn, for clearly her husband had fallen prey to the Unktehi. To be married to a little rabbit or a sad dog was an unfortunate fate indeed. It was definitely grounds for divorce.

Feasts, ceremonies, and religious rituals played a large role in the life of the Teton Sioux. Disputes were settled and important decisions made by special tribal councils.

Winter was a time of rest for the Teton Sioux. It was a time to wrap oneself in a buffalo robe and to sleep a lot—surrounded by one's family in the comfort of the warm tipis and lodges. It was a time for the women to decorate shirts, leggings, and dresses, and to make cradles for pregnant wives. It was a time for the men to work on bows and arrows and other weapons. It was a time to gather around the fire pit in the tipi or the lodge, to eat delicious pemmican (preserved buffalo meat spiced with herbs), to frolic with the children, and to play games. Most of all, it was a time to tell stories. Many a winter's cold gray day or black, icy night was passed telling stories. The Teton Sioux had many stories. Some favorites were told again and again. One of these was the tale of The Woman Who Lived with the Wolves.

One winter, a young Teton Sioux wife argued with her husband. Angrily, she took a little food and ran out onto the plains. Soon her food was gone. Night was falling, and she was very cold and tired. Discovering a cave, she crawled inside. She was shivering from the cold, but she was so tired that she fell asleep anyway. Later, in the middle of the night, the young woman awoke. To her surprise, she was very warm and comfortable. Reaching out with her hands, she felt soft, warm fur pressing all around her. Surrounded by warmth, she was soon asleep again.

In the morning, the young woman awoke to find wolves sleeping all around her. She realized that she had gone to sleep in the den of a wolf pack. The wolves had snuggled up against her to keep her warm. A very large wolf then woke up and looked at her with its wolf eyes. The young woman became frightened then, for a wolf's eyes are mysterious. The winter twilight can be seen in a wolf's eyes. Wolves were strong medicine. But the big wolf said: "Don't be afraid. We are your friends. Are you hungry?"

"I'm starving," the young woman said. The large wolf then led his pack out to hunt. They returned with plenty of fresh deer meat. The young woman was so hungry that she ate the meat raw, much to the amusement of the wolves.

The young woman stayed with the wolves for two years. She played with the wolf pups and watched them grow. The pack hunted for her, protected her, gave her companionship, told her wolf stories and wolf jokes to pass the time, and kept her warm at night. One day, the large wolf told the young woman that it was time for her to return to her own people. He instructed her to follow a nearby herd of wild horses. The horses would lead her home. The young woman sadly said good-bye to the wolves. She found the wild horses and ran with them for two days. But when the wild horses came near to her home, the young woman decided that she wanted to stay with the horses. By this time, the young woman was wild herself.

Seeing the herd nearby, some men came out to capture horses. The horses were fast, and the woman was just as fast, running in the center of the herd where she could not be seen by the hunters. The Sioux men pursued the herd for days. When they finally roped a few horses, they found that they had roped a woman as well! The young woman struggled against them. She was as strong and swift as any pinto. But the men finally pulled her back to their camp along with a few wild horses.

When the young woman's hair was cut and she had been washed and clothed, everybody recognized her. After that, she stayed with her people. They had to closely watch her for a long time, for she had a wild look in her eyes. Sometimes she tried to run off again, especially when she heard a pack of wolves singing under the winter moon.

The Teton Sioux made their winter camps in the shadows of the sacred Black Hills. There they were sheltered from the harsh winters that swept across the Great Plains each year.

CHAPTER 4

Wakan Tanka

The Teton Sioux also journeyed to the Black Hills during the summer. The mysterious hills offered the tribe more than shelter from the cold winds of winter. For the Sioux, the Black Hills were sacred. In the Black Hills, the presence of Wakan Tanka is powerful.

The Sioux believe that the universe is many-in-one and one-in-many. Wakan Tanka is in all things, and all things are part of Wakan Tanka. The Black Hills are a place where Wakan Tanka is plentiful in all his variety. He dwells in the deep forests of shadow and sunshine. He makes his home in the cold, clear streams packed with fish. He can be found in the wolves, bears, deer, elk, wolverines, beavers, rabbits, squirrels, foxes, and coyotes. He can be heard in the music of many different birds singing and talking. He can be seen in the hawks and eagles circling above, as well as in the quiet life of plants and herbs and berries. And, at night, he makes himself known in the hoot of the owl and the song of the wolf and coyote, and in the moon and stars so clear and bright they seem low enough to reach up and touch.

In the Black Hills, Sioux emerging from their tipis into the mist of the quiet dawn are filled with Wakan Tanka, and the Sioux spirit is at peace. For here the Sioux experience the mystery of the oneness-and-the-many of Wakan Tanka and know that they too are part of the one-and-the-many.

In the late spring, the *Wakinsuzas* would decide it was time for the Sioux to move from their winter camp to higher ground. The Wakinsuzas were members of the council of tribal leaders known as the *Naca Ominicia*. Deciding when to break camp was one of the duties of the Wakinsuzas. Once a band of tiyospes was on the move, they also decided when to halt and where to set up a new camp.

At daybreak, the Wakinsuzas sent heralds throughout the lodges and tipis of the winter

continued on page 49

THE SACRED AND THE MUNDANE

This page and the seven that follow display various items used by the Teton Sioux. The items range from weapons of war to articles of clothing, from everyday tools to children's playthings. The Teton Sioux believed that the natural world and every aspect of human behavior had spiritual significance. The items pictured here are splendid examples of this belief. Like everything else in the Indians' lives, they combine the ceremonial with the commonplace, and beauty with usefulness. For the Teton Sioux, as for many other Native Americans, there was no difference between "religious" and "everyday" life. The world was a place of infinite mystery and spiritual power, and people believed that it was their responsibility to honor and respect the spirit world in everything they did. The ornaments and designs on such items as a pair of moccasins or a child's rattle do more than simply make the object colorful or pretty. They represent the sacred mystery that resides in all things, and they remind people of their place in the world.

Representations of a black buffalo with a fish on its side, two small birds, and a crane adorn the head of this Teton Lakota drum obtained by Mary Collins, a Christian missionary who lived with the Teton in the late 19th century.

The various pictographs on this Teton woman's dress, thought to date from 1840 to 1860, are believed to record either images from her dreams or her husband's exploits in battle.

This Teton child's moccasins are made of buckskin, with colored quills and beads used to create the tipi design on the vamp.

The beaded geometric designs on this pair of Teton moccasins for an adult male are intended as a representation of the four winds. According to anthropologist Ruth Underhill, "the nomadic Sioux . . . paid particular attention to the directions, the home of the four winds. Every object and every movement in a ceremony was oriented either toward the West, home of the buffalo; or the North, that of the purifying cold wind; or the East, whence wisdom comes; or the South, the warm country 'towards which we always face.' "

The two shields on these pages were intended for use in ceremonial dances rather than as protection in warfare. This shield, with pictographs of the night sky, rattlesnakes, a spider, a person, and an elk, probably belonged to a member of the Elk Dreamer society.

This shield was made for ceremonial use by a Teton named Fat Bear in the late 19th century. It was made from buckskin stretched over a rawhide frame; the attached feathers are from an eagle.

This vest and pants were intended for wear by a Teton boy. They date from approximately 1890.

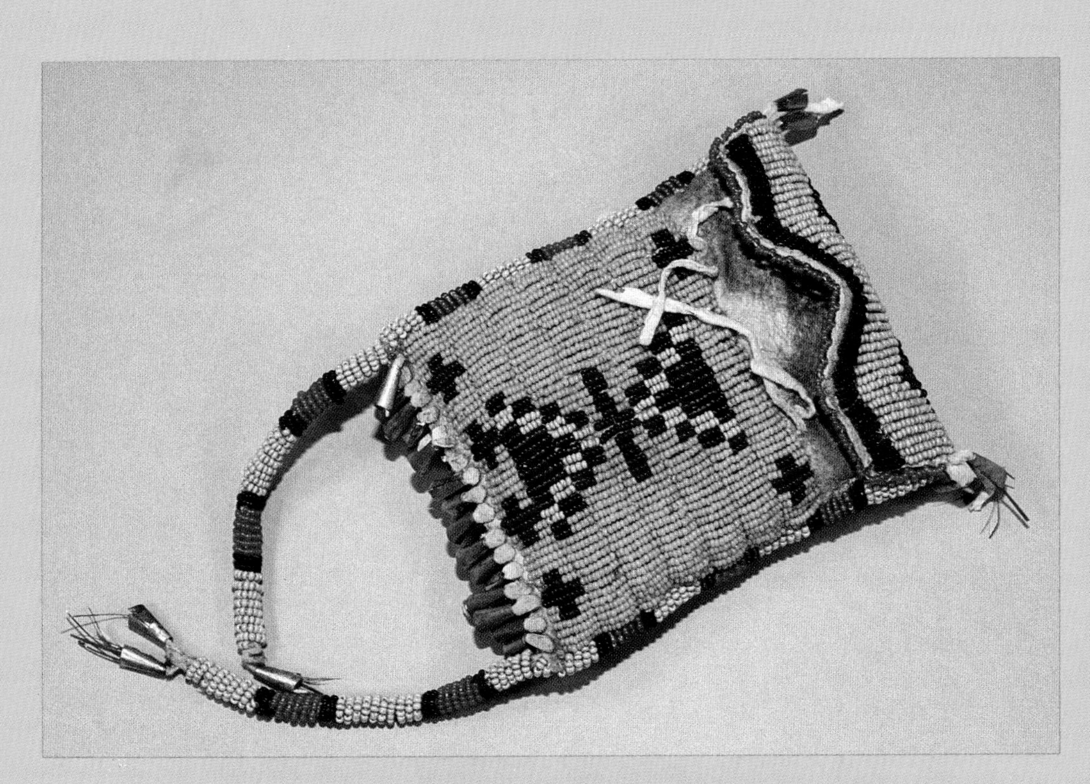

This small bag was used to carry tinder and material with which to start a fire.

The geometric designs on this Teton child's turtle fetish represent the four winds. The torso of the turtle was made of buckskin; the legs were made of rawhide and sewn to the body with animal sinew.

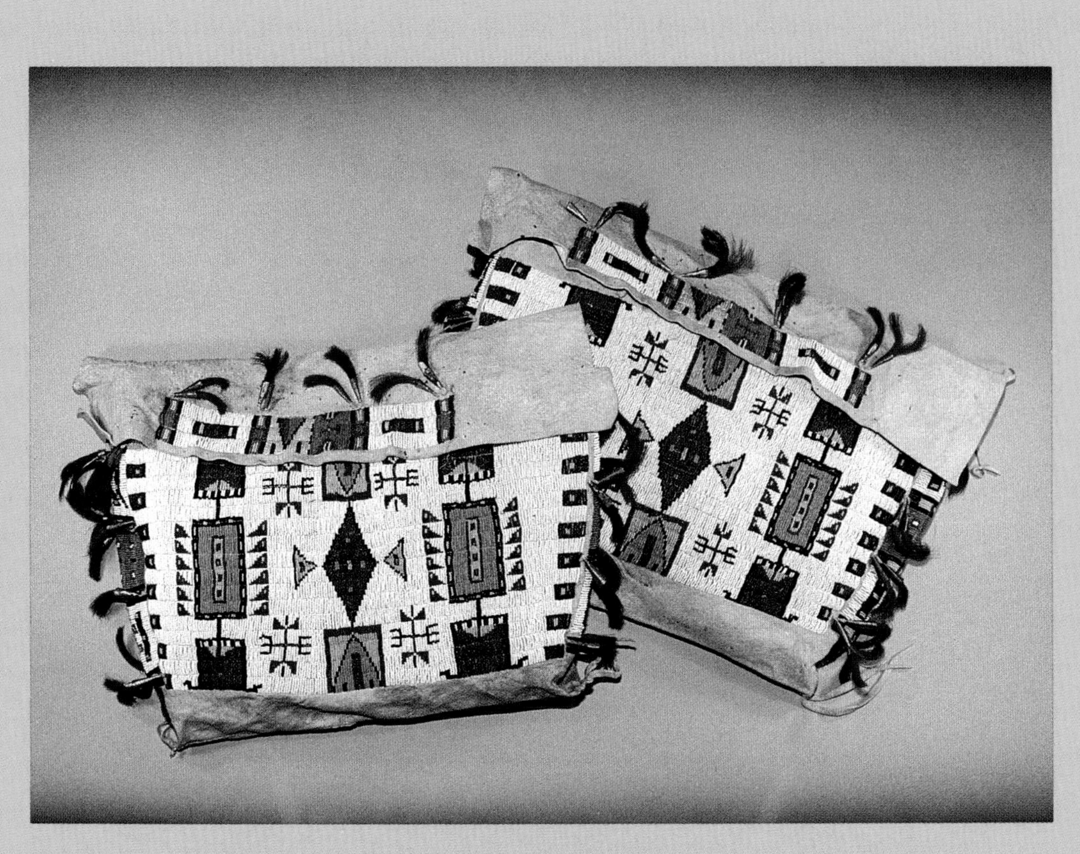

These buckskin tipi bags were used as all-purpose carriers by the Teton Lakota. They date from approximately 1895 and feature a common beaded design of various geometric shapes.

continued from page 40

village to announce the first move of spring. Although the tiyospes had been encamped for the entire winter, within 30 minutes their lodges and tipis would be dismantled and carefully folded away and packed. Their modest possessions were carried in deerskin and buffalo-skin sacks or loaded in bundles onto travois—sleds pulled by dogs and horses. Anything of value that was to be left behind was carefully buried. The hiding places were marked. Then the tiyospes would move in a single column, including many horses and dogs. It was a tight, disciplined column. Akicitas rode up and down the column, making sure that nobody strayed.

One winter, a band of Hunkpapa Teton Sioux camped in the Black Hills. Late in May, known to the Sioux as the Moon of the Thunderstorms, they moved to higher ground. On a warm evening, the Hunkpapa Sioux headman Tatanka Iyotake brought his *kola,* Gall, to a place he knew of high in the hills. Kolas were blood brothers. As boys, they were best friends. As they grew to be young men, they agreed to join together in all things—to be kolas. Kolas lived in the same tiyospe. They hunted together and went into battle together. Often, they married sisters. Kolas shared everything. Having a kola was

Although most tribal ceremonies focused on young males, women were highly respected members of the Sioux village. The young woman pictured here, Red Thing That Touches In Marching, wears the brightly decorated costume of an unmarried girl.

admirable in Teton Sioux society. It meant that there were always two instead of one. A man with a true kola was fortunate.

When Tatanka Iyotake was still hardly an adult himself, he adopted Gall, who was an orphan. At first, Tatanka Iyotake was a father figure to the boy. But eventually they became more like brothers. Now, they were kolas. As warriors, Tatanka Iyotake and Gall formed the most feared partnership in the history of all the tribes of the Great Plains.

On the evening that the two men climbed up into the high Black Hills, Tatanka Iyotake was still in his mid-twenties. But he was already a highly respected warrior and shaman among the Hunkpapa Teton Sioux. Eventually, he would emerge as the greatest of all the Teton Sioux leaders. In the history of white Americans, Tatanka Iyotake would be remembered by the English version of his Sioux name—*Sitting Bull.* Gall was already a true powerhouse of a young man. He was built like a buffalo, and he was as strong as one. Gall would become a feared warrior and a Teton Sioux leader himself.

Sitting Bull led Gall to a ridge high in the Black Hills. From there, one could overlook the entire northern Great Plains. This was the heart of the Teton Sioux Nation. A full moon bathed the plains in pale light. Looking in each direction, Sitting Bull and Gall observed the territory of the Seven Council Fires. Sitting Bull's gaze finally settled far to the northeast. That region, along the border of South Dakota and Minnesota, had once been the land of the Santee Sioux. The woodland Santees were the cousins of the Teton Sioux. But the Santees were no more. They had been destroyed by the Wasicu—the white man. (*Wasicu* was the Sioux term for white people. Its exact translation is "greedy ones.")

At first, the white people had trickled across the plains. They were passing

During the winters in the sacred hills, Sioux warriors often had dreams and visions of the spirit world. Ceremonies, such as the Deer Dreaming Ceremony (pictured here), celebrated the mystical nature of Sioux experience.

through, always headed west. The Sioux had befriended the whites. The Sioux had even guided them safely through the territory of the hostile Arikara tribe. But the trickle of whites eventually became a steady stream, then a rushing brook, then a river. Now the river overflowed its banks, and some whites began probing Teton Sioux land.

Many of the Teton Sioux leaders whom Sitting Bull spoke with were not worried about the whites. "There is enough room on the plains for all of us," some said. "We will make peace with them, and trade for guns and horses and tobacco and metal hatchets," said others. "They will come and we will kill many of them and they will not return," still others insisted. But Sitting Bull knew that things would not be so simple. The way of the white man and the way of the Sioux were as different as summer and winter. The two could never come together. There were many whites. And they were bad medicine. They destroyed the Santees. They killed off the buffalo in great numbers. They brought disease. Now they were building their forts in Oglala territory.

Sitting Bull and Gall had been standing on the high bluff for an hour. Neither had spoken. They were kolas, and so they were comfortable together in silence. A steady wind had risen. It was cool, blowing from the east. The wind grew stronger and colder. The moon disappeared. A streak of lightning illuminated the plains. For a brief moment, far in the distance, Sitting Bull saw a herd of buffalo stampeding away to the west. In the eastern sky, towering thunderclouds boiled and flickered. Jagged lightning cracked the sky. Thunder rolled across the plains toward the Black Hills. Sitting Bull and Gall stood in the face of the rising wind. "Come," Sitting Bull finally said. "We'll go back to camp. A storm is coming."

Chief Red Cloud was one of the great warriors who led the Sioux in their battles against the United States Army.

CHAPTER 5

"You Will Have To Fight the Sioux Warriors"

Following the end of the Civil War, white Americans poured westward in ever growing numbers. They were burning with the great national fever called *Manifest Destiny*. Manifest Destiny was the belief that North America, from the Atlantic Ocean in the East to the Pacific Ocean in the West, was destined to belong to white Christian "civilization." America, from sea to shining sea, would be "civilized" through exposure to the customs, the language, and the religion of the white settlers from Europe. The fact that these lands had been inhabited by other peoples for hundreds of years did not matter. There was no room for the original Americans in the white people's dream of Manifest Destiny.

At first, these westward-bound white Americans had traveled across the northern Great Plains along the Oregon Trail. This trail passed below Teton Sioux territory. Others heading west moved up the Missouri River, to the east and north of Teton Sioux country. But in 1866, the U.S. Army began building a series of forts along the Bozeman Trail. This road passed directly through Brulé and Oglala territory in Wyoming's Bighorn Mountain country. The Sioux watched as many bluecoats with cannons manned the forts. A Brulé chief, Standing Elk, rode down to the trail and confronted a force of 700 bluecoats as they were about to enter Oglala territory. He trotted his horse up to the leader of the force, Colonel Henry Carrington. "Where are you going?" asked Standing Elk. Carrington replied that he intended to protect white travelers heading to Montana on the Bozeman Trail. "You will have to fight the Sioux warriors," Standing Elk informed him.

Soon, Carrington and every other bluecoat in Oglala country were fighting the Sioux warriors. This was the first time the U.S. Army had encountered a large Teton Sioux army, instead of small bands of warriors. For two years, Oglala chief Red Cloud and 2,000 Oglala, Miniconjou, Brulé, and Hunkpapa warriors waged war along the Bozeman Trail. The Sioux were supported in their campaign by bands of Arapaho and Cheyenne allies.

One of the Oglalas, Crazy Horse, seemed to be everywhere. He lured the bluecoats into ambushes. He appeared suddenly with small bands of warriors in quick, hit-and-run attacks and then disappeared. He *taunted* bluecoat troops on the Bozeman Trail until they chased him off the road, only to find themselves suddenly surrounded by hundreds of Sioux warriors. Often he was glimpsed alone, shadowing a troop of soldiers like a spirit. Crazy Horse also coordinated several bloody, full-scale battles against bluecoat forces. In December 1866, Crazy Horse led a large party of Sioux and Arapahos that wiped out an entire regiment of bluecoat troops under the command of Captain William Fetterman.

Soon all the bluecoats learned to recognize Crazy Horse. His upper body was naked and painted with the images of hailstones. His hair was unusually light in color. He wore a single hawk's feather behind his head. A streak of lightning was painted down one high cheekbone. He rode a brown pinto. The soldiers were never happy to see him. And by spring 1868, the bluecoats had seen more than enough of the Teton Sioux and their allies. Too many bluecoats had lost their lives and their scalps. The Bozeman Trail had been shut down and the forts along the road isolated. No supplies could get through. Telegraph communications had been cut off.

The U.S. government decided that Manifest Destiny could just as well proceed *around* the Teton Sioux. In a treaty signed at Fort Laramie in Wyoming in December 1868, the United States government *renounced* forever any claims to Sioux territory in South Dakota west of the Missouri River and in the Bighorn Mountains of Wyoming and Montana. No white people would be allowed to enter this territory without permission of the Teton Sioux. The forts along the Bozeman Trail were abandoned. Then, one by one, the Sioux burned them to the ground. For the first time in the history of the United States, the American government had been forced to sign a treaty that represented a surrender.

The United States government had felt the power of the Teton Sioux Nation. But the Seven Council Fires had become the last obstacle standing between white America and its Manifest Destiny. By the 1870s, the

In 1874, gold was discovered in the Black Hills. The sudden arrival of miners and prospectors into the area meant that the Teton Sioux way of life had come to an end.

last pockets of Native American resistance were being crushed. The Teton Sioux Nation stood alone. It felt the medicine of white America surrounding it like a noose. The buffalo were disappearing; the great herds were being wiped out across the plains by white hunters. The railroads that passed close to Sioux hunting grounds frightened off other game. The wolves were fleeing to the forests of the northeast and Canada. Each winter, there were fewer buffalo robes and less food.

In 1874, gold was discovered in the Black Hills. Gold was the white man's most powerful medicine. It was so powerful that white men would do just about anything to get their hands on it. Small groups of miners had been sneaking into the Black Hills for years in search of gold. Most of them never returned from the Paha-Sapa alive, for Crazy Horse was at large. While these white men searched for gold, Crazy Horse searched for them.

But some of these gold miners did escape. Some of them had found gold. When the U.S. government got word of this, it attempted to buy mining rights to the Black Hills from the Teton Sioux. Some of the Sioux wanted to negotiate with the whites. Crazy Horse, by now recognized as the true voice of the Oglala Sioux, was disgusted by such talk. He informed the leaders of the Seven Council Fires that he personally would kill any Sioux who sold rights to the Black Hills. "One does not sell the earth upon which the people walk," Crazy Horse said. Sitting Bull, who was now the most powerful voice in the entire Teton Sioux Nation, had this to say: "We want no white men here. The Black Hills belong to me. If the whites try to take them, I will fight."

The United States government failed to honor the Fort Laramie Treaty. Just as they had done with hundreds of other agreements in the past, government leaders stuck by the terms of the treaty until they needed to break it. Gold in the Black Hills was more than enough reason to forget about any treaty with the Teton Sioux. In spring 1877, the U.S. Army invaded the Teton Sioux Nation. The Sioux were ready. They realized that they were now fighting not only for their land but for their way of life.

On June 17, 1876, 1,000 Cheyenne and Sioux warriors—led by Sitting Bull, Crazy Horse, and Chief Two Moons of the Cheyennes—rode out to meet an army of 1,200 bluecoats advancing under the command of General George Crook. The Sioux and Cheyennes attacked the bluecoats by Montana's Rosebud Creek. Crazy Horse coordinated

Though he was killed at the Battle of the Little Bighorn, General George Armstrong Custer was a highly respected fighter, even among his enemies in the Sioux Nation.

the warriors' strategy. He weakened Crook's superior numbers and firepower by dividing Crook's force into separate groups. After a day of savage fighting, Crook withdrew and retreated to the south to gather reinforcements. Crook was the best "Indian fighter" ever. Even the Indians had great respect for him. This was the first time that Crook had suffered a defeat. It was also the first time that he had encountered Crazy Horse.

The Sioux and Cheyenne forces then headed north to Sitting Bull's Hunkpapa village in the valley of the Little Bighorn River in Montana. On the way, they were joined by more Sioux, who had gotten word that another bluecoat force was approaching from the northeast. Sitting Bull's village was swollen with thousands of Hunkpapa, Oglala, Brulé, Miniconjou, Two Kettle, Sans Arc, Blackfeet, Cheyenne, Arapaho, and even some *refugee* Santee Sioux bands. Most of the warriors of the Teton Sioux Nation, their allies, and their tiyospes were encamped there.

On June 25, 1876, General George Armstrong Custer and the United States 7th Cavalry attacked Sitting Bull's village. Exactly why Custer did this has been debated by historians ever since. Custer had only about 200 cavalrymen; looking down from a bluff above Sitting Bull's village, he saw the largest gathering of warlike Indians ever assembled. But Custer was powerful medicine. At least he had been during the Civil War.

Had he been born 100 years later, George Armstrong Custer no doubt would have been a "top gun" commander of a jet-fighter or attack-helicopter squadron. General Custer was young and handsome. He was famous for the long, reddish blond hair that curled out from beneath his stylish white cavalryman's hat. (The Sioux called him Yellow Hair. The Sioux women thought he was quite handsome.)

In battle, Custer was daring and fearless. During the Civil War, the spectacular charges of Custer and the Union army's 7th Cavalry were legendary. They had turned the tide of many battles. Custer had passed through four years of fighting in that terrible conflict without a scratch. Numerous horses had been shot out from under him, but Custer himself—much like Crazy Horse—was untouched by bullets or cannon fire. Fighting against other white men, his medicine was strong. And Custer believed that white men were naturally superior to Indians. He also had political ambitions and an ego the size of Nebraska. Custer knew that if he won this battle, his name would be on the lips of every white person and in the headlines of every newspaper in the United States.

Custer charged. Two thousand, five hundred warriors, led by Gall and Crazy Horse, swarmed out of the village to meet the charge. Within 20 minutes, the Battle of the Little Bighorn was over. Custer and every man with him lay dead. It was as if the anger of every American Indian tribe ever mistreated by the white race had fallen on Custer and the 7th Cavalry.

White America was outraged. A great cry went up for the "final *extermination*" of the "savages" and "barbarians." But the Sioux had no feelings of *remorse* concerning the massacre. The United States had broken its treaty and invaded Sioux lands. They had acted dishonorably. This was no surprise to the Sioux. But they were perplexed by Custer's actions. Why had Yellow Hair, with only 200 soldiers, attacked such a powerful village? This was great foolishness, the Sioux felt. The Hunkpapa warrior Iron Hawk put it simply: "Those white men came to the Little Bighorn looking for trouble, and they found it."

6

The surrender of Sitting Bull at Fort Buford, North Dakota, in July 1881, broke the spirit of the Sioux resistance.

CHAPTER 6

The Heart of Crazy Horse

United States Army troops now invaded Teton Sioux territory in great numbers. New forts were built. The government was determined to destroy the Teton Sioux Nation once and for all. Avoiding large battles with the Sioux, the army instead harassed and divided the Sioux forces, destroyed Sioux food sources, and drove off or captured Sioux horses. Soon, the Teton Sioux could offer little resistance.

The winters were bitter times now. Food was scarce. The warriors were weakened and without horses. Babies and the elderly were dying. Messages were sent to the

Even in defeat, Crazy Horse was defiant. As he surrendered his band of warriors to the army at Fort Robinson, Nebraska, on May 6, 1877, he raised his rifle proudly into the air to show his lack of respect for his captors. Five months later, he was murdered while in custody by a soldier with a bayonet.

leaders of the Seven Council Fires. They were assured that, if they surrendered, they would be given plenty of food, warm clothes, and blankets. They would not be harmed. One by one, the leaders of the starving and *demoralized* Teton Sioux led their tribes to the forts to surrender.

On May 6, 1877, Crazy Horse led the ragged remnants of his band to Fort Robinson in Nebraska. Thousands of Teton Sioux who had surrendered were encamped in and around the fort. When they learned that Crazy Horse was coming, they lined the road to the fort's entrance and climbed to the top of the fort's walls, cheering, singing, and chanting Crazy Horse's name. Crazy Horse raised his rifle in the air in a final gesture of defiance.

He had surrendered, but he had never been defeated. Five months later, Crazy Horse was assassinated at Fort Robinson by a soldier with a bayonet. As he lay dying, he said to his father, "Tell the people it is no use to depend on me any more now." Crazy Horse was 35 years old. Later, his parents took Crazy Horse's heart and buried it in Oglala country somewhere near a creek known as Wounded Knee. The burial place was not marked.

Crazy Horse had always been a solitary soul. During his lifetime, he often disappeared into the hills by himself. He might be gone for weeks at a time before he reappeared. Nobody knew where he went during those periods, or what he did. The Oglala often called him *Ta-Shunka-Witco*—"the Strange One." Now he had disappeared forever. The entire Teton Sioux Nation mourned, and much of their spirit died with Crazy Horse.

Sitting Bull finally surrendered with his band of Hunkpapa in July 1881, at Fort Buford in North Dakota. He refused to hand over his rifle. Instead, he gave it to his son, who handed it to the officers. On December 15, 1890, Sitting Bull was assassinated by government agents outside his log cabin near Standing Rock, South Dakota.

Thirteen days later, the United States 7th Cavalry surrounded a band of 300 Miniconjou Sioux and their chief, Big Foot, near Wounded Knee Creek. The soldiers were sent to the *reservation* to suppress the *Ghost Dance,* a new spiritual movement that was spreading among the western reservations. When the cavalry appeared, a Miniconjou shaman named Yellow Bird began dancing the Ghost Dance. He was ordered to stop. Somebody fired a shot. The 7th Cavalry then opened fire on the Miniconjou camp. At least 300 Miniconjous—most of them elderly people, women, and children—were slaughtered, including Big Foot, one of the last true Teton Sioux chiefs. The blood of the Sioux turned the snow red.

The death of Sitting Bull and the horror of Wounded Knee seemed to kill the very soul of the Teton Sioux. They fell into a decline that was as rapid as their rise to power had been.

During the next 80 years, they continued to fall. The Black Hills were reclaimed by the United States. The land of the Sioux continued to disappear from beneath their feet. The reservation to which they had been assigned in North Dakota grew smaller and smaller and was eventually sliced into even smaller sections. First, ranchers helped themselves to large chunks, and then government energy agencies and private industrial corporations took their share.

The government policy of allotment ended collective tribal ownership of the land that was still left to the Sioux. Now, each Sioux adult male was given his own "private" piece of 160 acres of land. This policy did much to destroy the communal strength of the Teton Sioux culture. Sioux spiritual rituals such as the Sun Dance were declared illegal. Sioux children were taken from their parents and sent away to Christian boarding schools. At the schools, their hair was cut short. They were discouraged from speaking the Sioux language, from wearing traditional Sioux clothing, and from *thinking* like Sioux. Instead, they were taught how to become good "white" citizens. Poverty, unemployment, disease, depression, alcoholism, suicide, and violence took a terrible toll. By 1970, a government survey found that the Sioux reservations were the most impoverished communities in the United States and that the average life span of a Sioux male was less than 50 years.

And yet the Teton Sioux lived on. There was always a small group of Sioux who continued to practice the old ways in secret. They danced the Sun Dance. They

On February 28, 1973, a group of Indian activists, including many Teton Sioux, took over the tiny community of Wounded Knee, the site of the infamous massacre of 1890. Buddy Lamont, a Miniconjou-Oglala, was killed in the brief battle that followed with federal marshals.

performed the purifying *Sweat Lodge* ceremony. They went on *Vision Quests*, during which a young Sioux journeys alone to an isolated place and fasts for days until he enters a dream state, where he encounters his true self and discovers his role in life. They used the sacred *Calf Pipe*. The pipe was given to the Teton Sioux in the distant past by the Beautiful One, *Whope*, the daughter of the Sun and Moon. The pipe is smoked for friendship and community, for spiritual guidance in difficult times, and in order to be at one with the universe. And so the traditional ways survived, under the guardianship of those who knew that these things must not be lost.

In the early 1970s, the American Indian Movement (AIM) came to the Teton Sioux reservations. AIM was founded in Minneapolis, Minnesota, in 1968 by Eddie Benton Banai, George Mitchell, Clyde Bellecourt, and Dennis Banks. They were urban Indians, who had grown up in the "red ghettoes" of inner cities where impoverished Native Americans lived. AIM spread to the reservations, and soon it was at the forefront of a growing Indian rights movement in the United States.

AIM was embraced by many Teton Sioux, who were not only subjected to the worst living conditions imaginable on their reservations but who were also regularly victimized by violent and corrupt thugs hired by the Bureau of Indian Affairs to police the reservations. On February 28, 1973, AIM activists and hundreds of Oglala men and women took over the tiny community of Wounded Knee. They were soon joined by allies from numerous tribes around the country. Within two days, Wounded Knee was surrounded by an army of officers from the Federal Bureau of Investigation (FBI), assisted by federal marshals and local "volunteers." An 80-day confrontation followed. The standoff included periods of heavy gunfire from both sides. There was one death. Buddy Lamont, a Miniconjou-Oglala, was killed by a bullet to the head. Lamont was a Vietnam War volunteer. His great-aunt and great-uncle had been killed in the massacre of Big Foot's people at Wounded Knee in 1890.

AIM, the Sioux, and their allies surrendered in May. Their action had drawn the attention of not only the people of the United States but of the entire world. Another controversial and highly publicized episode occurred in June 1975, when a shoot-out between FBI agents, a number of Sioux, and AIM activists on the Oglala Pine Ridge reservation resulted in the death of two agents. Leonard Peltier, an Ojibwa-Sioux, was convicted of murder in the case, although he was clearly not guilty. Efforts to appeal the conviction of Leonard Peltier continue to this day.

By the 1980s, AIM had been broken by the government. Its members were scattered, in jail, on the run, or in hiding. But AIM seemed to awaken many Teton Sioux. Increasing numbers of Sioux began turning back to the traditional lifeways and spiritualism. The Teton Sioux also stepped up their lawsuit against the government for the return of the Black Hills. Currently, the government is offering a cash settlement for the Black Hills.

But most of the Teton Sioux favor holding out for the return of the hills themselves. Crazy Horse would have approved.

The Sioux reservations are still plagued by poverty, alcoholism, dismal health care, racism, and despair. Can a once-thriving people recover from such a long and hard fall? The fact that the Teton Sioux have survived at all indicates that they will find themselves again. And, like a young warrior on a Vision Quest, they will know their role as the new century approaches. Let us hope so, for there is much to learn from these people, especially in these times. Our polluted and poisoned environment is dying around us, our sense of community has become confused, and, in many ways, our spirituality has been lost. Ironically, soon America will need the Teton Sioux. The Sioux certainly owe nothing to America, but they are traditionally a generous people. And they are strong medicine.

GLOSSARY

demoralized discouraged; brokenhearted

extermination getting rid of a group completely by killing off every member

Ghost Dance a religion started in the late 1800s that predicted the end of the world, followed by a return to the traditional Native American way of life

harass to bother with repeated attacks

impose to force something upon another

nomadic moving from place to place, depending on the food supply or the season, and setting up temporary camps

refugee one who flees to another area to escape danger

remorse sense of guilt and regret for one's actions

renounce to give up, refuse, or resign by formal declaration

reservation a tract of land set aside by the U.S. government for a specific group of Native Americans to use

ritual a ceremony, usually following religious or social customs

shaman a wise "medicine man" able to heal the sick or see the future

stoicism lack of response to pain or pleasure

Sweat Lodge a ceremony during which people sweat away their impurities to prepare for other sacred rituals

taunt to challenge in a mocking, insulting way

tipi an easily movable, cone-shaped home made of buffalo hides and wooden poles

Vision Quest a sacred ritual in which a person fasts and prays alone for four days to receive guiding visions from the spirits

Wakan Tanka the Creator and Great Spirit, who is in everyone and everything

CHRONOLOGY

ca. 1735 The Sioux move westward from present-day Minnesota and Wisconsin and then split up; the Teton Sioux settle in the northern Great Plains of present-day North and South Dakota

1795 Teton Sioux win control of the Black Hills from the Kiowas and continue westward into present-day Montana and Wyoming; they divide into seven tribes

1866 U.S. Army builds forts to protect American settlers traveling through Sioux territory on the Bozeman Trail; Red Cloud and Crazy Horse lead Sioux warriors in battles against the army

1868 Forts on Bozeman Trail abandoned; United States signs Fort Laramie Treaty giving up its claims to Sioux land

1870s White hunters slaughter huge herds of buffalo, creating a lack of food for the Sioux; railroads run through Sioux territory

1874 Gold discovered in Black Hills attracts whites to the area; Crazy Horse and Sitting Bull warn the Sioux not to sell sacred land

1876 United States breaks Fort Laramie Treaty and attacks the Teton Sioux Nation; led by Crazy Horse and Gall, the Sioux kill Custer and all his soldiers at the Battle of the Little Bighorn

1877 Army attacks and food shortages force many weakened Sioux to surrender; Crazy Horse assassinated by a U.S. soldier

1881 Sitting Bull and his followers surrender

1890 Sitting Bull killed by government agents; U.S. government tries to stop Ghost Dance; army massacres more than 300 Sioux near Wounded Knee

early 1900s Teton Sioux lose much of their land, including the Black Hills, to government agencies and private businesses; traditional Sioux ways outlawed by U.S. government

1973 American Indian Movement (AIM) leads 80-day takeover of Wounded Knee

1975 Shoot-out between FBI agents and AIM members on Sioux Pine Ridge reservation

1980s Teton Sioux file lawsuit against U.S. government for return of Black Hills; more and more Sioux practice their traditional customs and spiritual beliefs

INDEX

A
Akicita societies, 21, 29, 49
Allotment policy, 71
American Indian Movement (AIM), 73, 74
Arapaho Indians, 24, 57, 63
Arikara Indians, 17, 23, 52

B
Badgers, 21
Banai, Eddie Benton, 73
Banks, Dennis, 73
Bellencourt, Clyde, 73
Big Foot (Miniconjou chief), 70, 74
Blackfeet Teton Sioux Indians, 24, 63
Black Hills, 10, 24, 25, 32, 33, 39, 51, 60, 61, 70, 74–75
Bozeman Trail, 56, 57, 58
Brulé Teton Sioux Indians, 24, 56, 57, 63
Buffalo, 8, 11, 14, 15, 18, 19, 27, 28, 32, 33, 53, 60
Bureau of Indian Affairs (BIA), 73

C
Calf Pipe, 72
Cheyenne Indians, 24, 57, 61, 63
Chippewa Indians, 9
Civil War, 64
Counting coup, 20–21
Crazy Horse (Oglala chief), 23, 57, 60–65, 68–69, 75
Cree Indians, 23
Crook, George, 61, 63
Crow Indians, 17, 24, 28, 29
Crow Owners, 21
Custer, George Armstrong, 63–65

D
Dakota Sioux Indians, 9. *See also* Santee Sioux Indians

F
Federal Bureau of Investigation (FBI), 73, 74
Fetterman, William, 57
Fort Buford, North Dakota, 69
Fort Laramie, Wyoming, 58
Fort Laramie Treaty, 58, 61
Fort Robinson, Nebraska, 68, 69

G
Gall (Hunkpapa chief), 21, 49–53, 65
Ghost Dance, 70
Great Plains, 9, 10, 11, 14, 15, 23, 25, 33, 50, 56

H
Hunkpapa Teton Sioux Indians, 24, 49, 51, 57, 63, 65, 69

I
Iron Hawk, 65
Iroquois Confederacy, 9, 25

K
Kiowa Indians, 17, 24
Kit Foxes, 21

L
Lakota Sioux Indians, 9. *See also* Teton Sioux Indians
Lamont, Buddy, 74
Little Bighorn, Battle of the, 63–65

M
Miniconjou Teton Sioux Indians, 24, 57, 63, 70, 74
Minnesota, 8, 9, 10, 51
Missouri River, 9, 24, 56, 58
Mitchell, George, 73
Montana, 9, 24, 64, 68

N
Naca Ominicia, 40
Nakota Sioux Indians, 9
Nebraska, 9, 24, 64, 68
North Dakota, 9, 69, 70

O
Oglala Teton Sioux Indians, 24, 56, 57, 60, 63, 69, 73, 74
Ojibwa Indians, 24
Omaha Indians, 24
Oregon Trail, 56

P
Pawnee Indians, 17, 23, 28
Peltier, Leonard, 74
Pemmican, 34
Pine Ridge reservation, 74
Ponca Indians, 24

R
Red Cloud (Oglala chief), 57

S
Sans Arc Teton Sioux Indians, 24, 63
Santee Sioux Indians, 9, 51, 53, 63
Seven Council Fires, 24, 25, 30, 32, 51, 58, 61, 68
Shamans, 15, 30
Shoshone Indians, 17, 23, 28
Sitting Bull (Hunkpapa chief), 49–53, 61, 63, 69, 70. *See also* Tatanka Iyotake
South Dakota, 9, 51, 58, 69
Spanish conquistadores, 10, 11
Standing Elk (Brulé chief), 56
Strong Hearts, 21
Sun Dance, 30, 32, 71
Sweat Lodge ceremony, 72

T
Tatanka. *See* Buffalo
Tatanka Iyotake, 49–53. *See also* Sitting Bull
Teton Sioux Indians. *See also* Lakota Sioux Indians
  and buffalo, 8, 11, 14–15, 18, 27, 28, 32, 33, 53, 60
  genesis myth, 9–10
  and horses, 17, 18, 19, 28, 52, 67
  language, 71
  religion, 8, 9–10, 11–13, 15, 39–40, 70, 71, 72, 74
  on reservations, 70–75
  today, 67–75
  treaties, 58, 65
  warfare, 17–24, 55–65
  warrior societies, 21, 29, 49
  war with U.S., 55–65
  way of life, 27–53, 71
  women, 28, 34, 35–37, 64
Tiyospes, 27, 28, 32, 33, 40, 49, 63
Two Kettle Teton Sioux Indians, 24, 63
Two Moons (Cheyenne chief), 61

V
Vision Quests, 72, 75

W
Wakan Tanka (Great Spirit), 8, 11, 13, 14, 32, 39, 40
Wakinsuzas, 40
Warrior societies. *See* Akicita societies
Wisconsin, 8, 9, 10
Woman Who Lived with the Wolves, The, 35–37
Wounded Knee, South Dakota
  massacre, 70, 74
  occupation of, 73
Wyoming, 9, 24, 56, 58

Y
Yankton Sioux Indians, 9
Yellow Bird, 70

ABOUT THE AUTHOR

TERRANCE DOLAN is a writer, editor, and bat enthusiast living in Brooklyn, New York.

PICTURE CREDITS

Library of Congress: p. 66 (neg. #Z62-19837); Little Bighorn Battlefield National Monument: p. 62; From the collection of the Minnesota Historical Society: pp. 26–27; National Anthropological Archives, Smithsonian Institution: p. 2 (neg. #3193-A); National Museum of American Art, Washington, DC/Art Resource, NY: pp. 6, 8, 12, 22, 30–31, 50; The Research Libraries, New York Public Library: pp. 20, 34, 52, 68; South Dakota State Archives: pp. 38, 54, 59; South Dakota State Historical Society, Pierre/Photos by Robert Travis: pp. 41, 42, 43, 44, 45, 46, 47, 48; UPI/Bettmann: p. 72; Walters Art Gallery, Baltimore: pp. 16–17.